Dear Parents:

Congratulations! Your child is taking the first steps on an exciting journey. The destination? Independent reading!

STEP INTO READING® will help your child get there. The program offers five steps to reading success. Each step includes fun stories and colorful art or photographs. In addition to original fiction and books with favorite characters, there are Step into Reading Non-Fiction Readers, Phonics Readers and Boxed Sets, Sticker Readers, and Comic Readers—a complete literacy program with something to interest every child.

Learning to Read, Step by Step!

Ready to Read **Preschool–Kindergarten**
• big type and easy words • rhyme and rhythm • picture clues
For children who know the alphabet and are eager to begin reading.

Reading with Help **Preschool–Grade 1**
• basic vocabulary • short sentences • simple stories
For children who recognize familiar words and sound out new words with help.

Reading on Your Own **Grades 1–3**
• engaging characters • easy-to-follow plots • popular topics
For children who are ready to read on their own.

Reading Paragraphs **Grades 2–3**
• challenging vocabulary • short paragraphs • exciting stories
For newly independent readers who read simple sentences with confidence.

Ready for Chapters **Grades 2–4**
• chapters • longer paragraphs • full-color art
For children who want to take the plunge into chapter books but still like colorful pictures.

STEP INTO READING® is designed to give every child a successful reading experience. The grade levels are only guides; children will progress through the steps at their own speed, developing confidence in their reading.

Remember, a lifetime love of reading starts with a single step!

P9-BZG-501

For Mary and Robin
—C.C.

Copyright © 2019 Disney Enterprises, Inc. All rights reserved. Published in the United States by Random House Children's Books, a division of Penguin Random House LLC, 1745 Broadway, New York, NY 10019, and in Canada by Penguin Random House Canada Limited, Toronto, in conjunction with Disney Enterprises, Inc.

Step into Reading, Random House, and the Random House colophon are registered trademarks of Penguin Random House LLC.

Visit us on the Web!
StepIntoReading.com
rhcbooks.com

Educators and librarians, for a variety of teaching tools, visit us at RHTeachersLibrarians.com

ISBN 978-0-7364-3985-5 (trade) — ISBN 978-0-7364-8276-9 (lib. bdg.)
ISBN 978-0-7364-3986-2 (ebook)

Printed in the United States of America

10 9 8 7 6 5 4 3 2 1

Disney
THE
LION KING

by Courtney Carbone
illustrated by the Disney Storybook Art Team

Random House 🏠 New York

A lion cub is born
in the Pride Lands.
Simba is the son
of King Mufasa
and Queen Sarabi.
He is next to be king!

Everyone is excited
about Simba—
except his uncle Scar.
Scar is jealous.
He wants to be
the next king!

Time passes.

Simba grows older.

He loves to explore

with his friend Nala.

Mufasa teaches his son everything he knows. Simba cannot wait to be king!

Scar has other plans.
He pushes Mufasa
off a steep cliff!
Scar blames Simba.

He tells the little cub
to run away.

Simba is scared.

He runs away.

Scar becomes
the new king.
But he is nothing
like Mufasa.

Simba begins a new life
far from home.
His new friends are
Timon and Pumbaa.

Timon and Pumbaa
take good care
of Simba.

Soon he grows
into a big, strong lion.
Simba is happy.
But he cannot
forget his past.

One day, a
lioness arrives.
She tries to eat
Pumbaa!

Simba stops her
just in time.
Then he realizes
the lioness is Nala!

Nala cannot believe
she found Simba!
They are so happy
to see each other.

Simba agrees to go
back home with Nala.
It is time to take his
place as king.

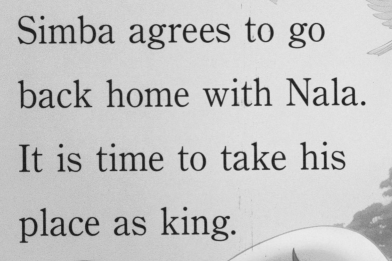

Simba returns
to the Pride Lands.
Scar tells Simba that
<u>he</u> pushed Mufasa.

Simba is furious.
He fights his uncle
and wins.

At last, Simba is king!
He and Nala begin
a new Circle of Life
together.

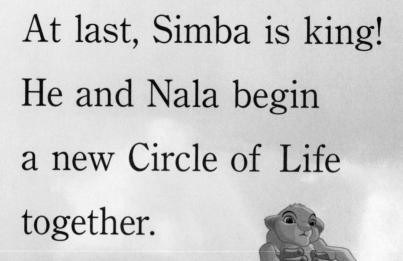